REVIEWS OF
MILO AND ONE DEAD ANGRY DRUID

'Gripping stuff for age eight-plus and its lively style makes it a good bet with reluctant readers.'

Evening Echo

'Brilliantly written with clever humour and twists and turns.'

Woman's Way

'Exciting supernatural adventure ... great humour, pace and cliffhangers that will keep young readers turning the pages and looking forward to more in the series.'

Children's Books Ireland Recommended Reads Guide 2013

Mary Arrigan studied at the National College of Art and Design, Dublin, and at Florence University. She became a full-time writer in 1994. Her novel for teenagers *The Rabbit Girl*, one of her forty-four published books, was selected by the United States Board on Books for Young People for their list of Outstanding International Books for 2012. Her awards include the International White Ravens title, a Bisto Merit Award, a *Sunday Times*/Crime Writers' Association Award and a Hennessy Literary Award. Her books have been translated into twelve languages. You can read more Milo Adventures in *Milo and One Dead Angry Druid*, *Milo and the Raging Chieftains*, and *Milo and the Long Lost Warriors*.

THE MILO ADVENTURES

MILO AND THE PIRATE SISTERS

WRITTEN AND ILLUSTRATED BY

MARY ARRIGAN

THE O'BRIEN PRESS
DUBLIN

First published 2014 by The O'Brien Press Ltd.,
12 Terenure Road East, Rathgar, Dublin 6, Ireland.
Tel: +353 1 4923333; Fax: +353 1 4922777
E-mail: books@obrien.ie
Website: www.obrien.ie

ISBN: 978-1-84717-562-5

Layout and design: The O'Brien Press Ltd.
Cover illustrations: Neil Price
Printed and bound by CPI Group (UK) Ltd, Croydon, CR0 4YY
The paper in this book is produced using pulp from
managed forests.

The O'Brien Press receives financial assistance from

For Conor and Marcella

Thanks to my excellent editor, Susan Houlden, and to my husband, Emmet, for his patient input and suggestions.

CONTENTS

CHAPTER ONE

BAD NEWS

'Rain, Milo,' Shane groaned, pulling his football shorts out of his sports bag and putting them over his head. 'What awful thing did the ancient Irish people do to this country to turn it into a giant loo that's always flushing?'

'That's gross,' I said, jumping over a puddle and landing on one foot in the middle of it. 'But,' I added defensively, 'it's the rain that makes Ireland so green. People come from all over the world to see the amazing scenery.'

'Greenery me eye,' Shane laughed as he jumped in the same puddle and splashed my other leg. 'Whoever planned the earth must have been so fed up by the time they got to Ireland that they just dumped all the leftover dirty rain clouds here and then scarpered.'

That so annoyed me, but I couldn't think of any brilliant words because I was focusing on my squelchy wet feet.

We were heading home from football training. It's not that we're hoping to be soccer trillionaires, it's just that we figure it makes us look kinda macho. We steer clear of the ball and the mad guys who steamroll after it. Best of all, it gets us out of boring chores at home.

'Think of it, Milo,' Shane went on, holding out a hand to catch raindrops. 'Gran told me that when we lived in Africa when I was a baby, people had to walk miles for water. They still do. Wouldn't it be great if we could invent something that would whoosh buckets of those watery clouds over to Africa and sweep months of sunshine back here?'

I stopped and looked at him, the legs of his football shorts flapping over his head like elephant ears and the raindrops bouncing on his coffee-coloured face.

'What are you laughing at?' he scowled.

'You, of course! Come on, we'll nip through the castle side-gate and have a hot chocolate with Mister Lewis.'

'Smart thinking, Milo.' Shane's scowl changed to a grin and he patted his fat tum.

Our good friend Mister Lewis once lived in Shane's old house until he died. That was over a hundred years ago, when he had a fatal run-in with a very unpleasant character. Now, as a sort of half-ghost, Mister Lewis was living in the derelict tower that's across the courtyard from the town castle. When Shane pushed open the creaky door, there was a very scary screeching sound, followed by loud wailing that echoed eerily down the winding stairs.

'It's only me and Shane,' I shouted up.

'Ah,' the voice changed to normal. 'Come on up, lads. Mind the holes on the stairs.'

Not that we needed his warning; we were well used to going up those stairs to the very top where no one ever ventured because it was rumoured that it was haunted. Which was true, of course. Mister Lewis can do a really mean, gurgling death rattle that would scare the toughest trespassers.

He was already putting on the woolly gloves that Shane's granny, Big Ella, had given him. Being a halfway sort of ghost, you see, his hands would just go through things if he didn't wear the gloves. As usual, his putty-coloured face lit up when we opened the door. He had already lit the little gas ring Big Ella had given him along with some Bart Simpson mugs. She insisted that, ghost or no ghost, he must have at least a warm drink inside him.

'Score any goals, lads?' he asked as he stirred drinking chocolate into the heating milk and then added a spoonful of honey from the friendly bees that had settled up in the rafters.

'Nearly,' said Shane. 'Just missed the post.'

'That's because you were at the wrong goalpost,' I laughed.

Strangely, Mister Lewis didn't laugh like he always does when we tell him fun stuff. He just sighed as he poured the hot chocolate from Big Ella's saucepan into the mugs and handed them to us. We sat down on her squishy scatter cushions.

'Ah,' Mister Lewis sighed again, easing himself carefully onto the biggest one. 'What a lucky old ghost I am. I have had every comfort up here in my tower and, most of all, I have two very good friends.' Then there was another sigh. Was the hot chocolate oozing into his brain and making him go soft in the head?

'You're talking a bit weird, Mister Lewis,' said Shane. 'Your mouth is down and your eyes are foggy.'

'Shane's right,' I added. 'And you're talking in the past tense, like "had" instead of "have". You're not ...' I gulped. 'You're not dying or anything, are you?'

'He's always been dead, you dope,' whispered Shane. 'At least for as long as we've known him.'

Mister Lewis waved his hand around the room that Big Ella, Shane and myself had made cosy for him. We had even found him a statue of a ginger cat in a skip. Shane said that old people like cats – especially ones that sit still and don't wee or cough up furballs.

'My lovely home,' Mister Lewis whispered. 'I heard the castle authorities mooching around downstairs yesterday. They were discussing a makeover for the tower.' He stopped and took a big, spooky breath. 'They're going to strip the tower and do it up to make it part of the whole castle complex.'

'No way!' Shane exploded.

'For real?' I put in.

'Afraid so,' Mister Lewis sighed. 'I must move out before they start work on it the day after tomorrow.'

'That means—?' I began.

'It means, my dear, good friends, that I shall be homeless.'

CHAPTER TWO

WEDGE AND CRUNCH

'What will we do, Milo?' Shane asked on our way home from school next day. 'Poor dead man with no home. Couldn't he hide at your place?'

I stopped and looked at him. 'Are you serious? My mum would freak out and run screaming down the road in her pyjamas, and my dad would sling him in jail for scaring folks with his corpse-coloured face and creepy old hat. Couldn't he live with you and Big Ella? After all, she knows him well and she isn't spooked.'

Shane's lip curled downwards. 'We've only two bedrooms,' he muttered.

'You could share,' I put in. 'He could sleep under your bed.'

'No way,' snapped Shane. 'All my precious stuff is under there.'

'Like what?' I asked.

'Old stuff,' he muttered.

'What old stuff, Shane?'

'Just stuff, OK?' he grumped.

'Your old toys?' I laughed. 'It's where you keep your old toys!'

'Mind your own business,' Shane muttered and headed off down the road like a gigantic soccer ball in motion. I watched him for a few moments. This wasn't right. Good pals shouldn't be like this. But before I could call him, two familiar guys came around the bend. I groaned out loud. They were our old enemies, Wedge and Crunch from sixth class – like, whenever they actually came to school. Wedge grabbed Shane's jacket and Crunch was already searching the pockets. Well, you don't stand around and watch your best mate being mauled by a couple of low-lifes. So I ran to help him.

'Hey!' I shouted – well, to be honest, it was really more of a shaky croak. 'You guys leave my buddy alone.' I nearly added 'please', but they would just laugh. These two guys don't do polite.

'Ha,' grinned Wedge. 'The skinny weasel has come to rescue his roly-poly pal.'

'Aww,' sneered Crunch as he grabbed my jacket and pulled me so close to his skinny nose I could see snot getting ready to dribble.

'Hey,' he laughed. 'Ain't you the little gentleman?'

'Hey,' said another voice, a voice we knew so well – Mister Lewis! He came around the corner wheeling a supermarket trolley, filled high with his stuff. On top of the lot was a large, decorative paper bag.

'Good day to you, boys,' he said. 'Having a nice chat together?'

'None of your business, old man,' sneered Wedge.

'What's in the fancy bag?' asked Crunch, reaching towards it.

'I don't think you should touch ...' began Mister Lewis. Before he could finish, Crunch snatched the bag, laughing as he ran down the road shaking it.

'Wait for me!' shouted Wedge, running after his greedy mate.

Mister Lewis shook his head. 'Oh dear,' he whispered.

The screams came first, followed by a blurry cloud of bees that buzzed angrily over Wedge and Crunch – mostly Crunch, because Wedge had pulled his hoodie over his head. They turned and ran back towards us, flapping their hands and shouting at Mister Lewis for help as they passed.

'But what about your bees, Mister Lewis?' asked Shane. 'Those guys will stamp them into the ground!'

'Not at all, boy,' said Mister Lewis. 'My buzzing friends will come back to me when I get to our new dwelling place.'

'Where?' I asked. 'The castle is out of bounds now, and there are no other places where a ghost could live.'

Mister Lewis stopped and tapped his

nose (gently, because bits fall off if he's not careful). 'Well,' he began, 'thanks to an old history of the town that I found on one of my nightly visits to the castle library, I think I have found the solution to my, eh, situation. I hope both of you, my two best friends – indeed, along with Big Ella, you are my only living friends – will help me. It's not very far.'

'Of course we will,' we said together.

'We'll give you any help we can,' I said.

'Any help at all,' added Shane, just to get in the last word.

CHAPTER THREE

WONKY TROLLEY

'Where did you get the trolley?' asked Shane, as we walked towards the town.

'I borrowed it,' Mister Lewis chuckled.

'You nicked it?' I exclaimed. 'If you're caught—!'

'Oh, I won't be caught,' he said. 'But you boys make sure *you're* not caught.'

'Us?' put in Shane. 'What do you mean?'

'Well, you have offered to help,' said Mister Lewis.

'Why can't you just go invisible and push the trolley?' I asked.

'How do you think that would look, Milo?' Mister Lewis went on. 'A full trolley steering its way through the town all by itself?'

Well, he had a point. There was no answer to that.

'So will you help me, boys? We're close to town and I have to go invisible in case old ladies faint or cars crash, or my nose wobbles or I accidentally waft off the ground, or—'

'All right, Mister Lewis,' I interrupted. 'We'll do it. But you'd better stick around.'

'No worries,' said Mister Lewis.

'I wish I could go invisible too,' Shane whispered. 'Especially if someone squeals to Big Ella that I was up to no good with a supermarket trolley full of stuff.'

'What about me?' I hissed into Shane's ear.

You see, my dad is a Garda. Imagine having to haul your own son before some judge with a face like broken granite. My dad says judges have to have granite faces before they can qualify to wear those woolly wigs made from sheep's ringlets.

So Mister Lewis did go invisible, which made good sense: how would me and Shane explain why we were walking along the busy street with a waxy-faced man wearing a long, dusty old coat and crooked hat, wheeling a supermarket trolley full of junk? The only scare was when we took a short-cut past the old abandoned knickers factory. The wee-waw of a speeding Garda car caused me and Shane to duck, but luckily my dad wasn't in it – the Garda car, I mean, not the knickers factory. When we'd left the town, Mister Lewis appeared again, sitting on top of the stuff in the trolley. He yawned and stretched his skinny arms.

'Ah, that was a grand sleep. Thanks, lads.'

'You mean we've been pushing you all the way?' spluttered Shane. 'Cheek!'

'But I weigh nothing at all,' laughed Mister Lewis as he wafted off the trolley.

'Cool,' Shane laughed. 'I wish I could weigh nothing at all.'

'And miss Big Ella's awesome cakes and buns?' I put in.

Shane patted his roundy tummy. 'Hmm. Maybe not,' he grinned.

CHAPTER FOUR

A VIEW FROM THE BRIDGE

Beyond the town, we stopped just before the bridge across the river.

'Here we are,' said Mister Lewis.

'Is this it?' asked Shane. 'You're going to live in the river? I know you're a kinda ghost, Mister Lewis, but you shouldn't need to live with fishes.'

'Fishes, Shane? Look over there,' Mister

27

Lewis went on, pointing farther up the river.

'The old mill? I exclaimed. 'It's a bit ...' I couldn't think of a single comforting word.

'It's a dump.' Trust Shane to be upfront about it. 'A total dump, Mister Lewis. And scary,' he added. 'Nobody goes there, ever.'

He was right. From here the mill looked derelict. The big wheel was falling apart and there were slates missing from the roof.

Mister Lewis sighed and shook his head. 'This was built after my, eh, sudden death,' he said. 'How very strange that it's already in ruins. Mills were built to last a long time. I saw it for the first time only yesterday. See, it has decent walls and some of the roof looks quite OK.'

'Did you go inside?' I asked.

'No, Milo,' he replied. 'I figured that if the outside is sound, the inside will be dry. And the scenery is quite picturesque,' he went on, pointing to the distant trees and a bunch of horses munching grass in a field.

'Yeah, all very pretty if it was a picture hanging on a wall, Mister Lewis,' I said. 'But as a place to live in? No way.'

'It will do, Milo,' he sighed. 'At least I'll have a roof of some sort over my head.'

'And hopefully over your toes,' said Shane. 'Big Ella goes mental about wet feet. It's to do with when we lived in Africa. She says people can get deadly diseases from dirty water.'

'I haven't actually seen my feet for well over a hundred years,' laughed Mister Lewis.

'That's gross,' I said. 'Don't they smell?'

'I don't know,' he replied. 'I've never had a reason to take off my boots – even if I could bend down that far.'

'You mean you haven't washed your feet since you died?' I exclaimed.

'Well, I hate having a bath too,' Shane put in. 'No matter what way I sit I nearly always get stuck. They make baths far too small,' he grunted.

'And perhaps they make crisps and chocolate far too big,' said Mister Lewis.

We all laughed at that.

We pushed the trolley down the road towards the bridge.

Mister Lewis stopped halfway across. 'See, boys,' he said, 'the mill's not so bad, looking at it from here. Some of those windows are not even broken.'

When we went along the track through the field towards the mill, Mister Lewis had to stop and sit down beside the trolley. 'I'm pooped,' he wheezed. 'Just give me a minute to crank up the old lungs.'

Shane and I ran over to where there were horses corralled and climbed onto the wooden gate. We were totally thrilled when the horses galloped over to us and let us pat their noses and ruffle their manes.

'This is so cool, Milo,' laughed Shane. 'I've never touched a horse's nose before. It feels like velvet.'

We patted each of them in turn as they jumped in front of one another to get our attention.

'This must be what a king feels like when his subjects dance all around him.' Shane beamed. 'I'd like to be a king. Where could you learn how to be a king, Milo?'

I laughed and shook my head. Sometimes Shane has the most amazingly mad ideas.

'Mister Lewis,' he called out, 'come and see the horses. They're so tame and friendly and their noses are made of velvet.'

Mister Lewis eased himself up and half walked and half wafted over. When he leaned on the gate, the strangest, creepiest thing happened. All the horses backed away in a sort of stomping panic. They jostled one another to get as far away as possible. Their shrill, screechy screams were so loud that we had to put our hands over our ears. They thundered away across the field, still snorting and kicking up grass and mud.

Mister Lewis shrugged his shoulders. 'Noisy creatures,' he muttered and headed back to the trolley.

Strangely enough, when he was gone the horses stopped whinnying.

CHAPTER FIVE

WEDGE AND CRUNCH AGAIN

Together we wheeled the trolley across the bumpy field towards the mill. There was a scruffy-looking boat moored in the river. We laughed when we saw the big, badly painted skull and crossbones flapping on a stick at the rear end of the boat. As we came nearer we could see two guys fishing. They were turned away from us, but there was no mistaking the backs of their bony heads.

'It's Wedge and Crunch!' exclaimed Shane.

'It's OK, Shane,' I said. 'You'll sort them out, won't you, Mister Lewis?'

We both looked around, but there was no sign of our ghostly buddy.

'Mister Lewis,' Shane hissed.

But there was still no sign of the only person who could sort out those two bullies.

'Quick!' said Shane, wobbling with fear. 'Let's move it.'

We tried to turn the trolley around, but it was too late. They'd spotted us. There was no point in running away as they'd catch us anyway because of the trolley.

'Well well, it's the dozy duo again,' said Wedge with a smirky smile. 'We'll have to stop meeting like this.'

They both put down their rods, hopped

off the boat and came towards us, Crunch waving a cheapo toy sword.

'Going for a picnic, guys?' Crunch called out, his bee-stung nose covered with green ointment.

'Yeah,' shouted Wedge. 'What's all that stuff in the stolen supermarket trolley? Tut, tut, Milo. Won't Daddy-the-cop throw a fit?'

As they came closer, Shane and myself stood together like a pair of clowns in a circus waiting for someone to throw a bucket of water over them. But the thing that hurt me the most was that Mister Lewis had abandoned us.

'Milo,' whispered Shane as I braced myself for the first whack.

'Shush,' I said through my clenched teeth. The enemy were almost on us.

'But Milo,' Shane hissed. 'Look behind!'

So I did, and my lungs began working

again when I saw a pair of dusty boots beginning to materialise. Just as Wedge grabbed my tee-shirt and Shane was being hassled by Crunch, the almost complete body of Mister Lewis rose up – apart from one side of his head, which was missing!

'Hello boys,' he said softly.

Wedge and Crunch froze, then screamed and ran like they'd seen a ghost – which is what they did see, of course.

'Wait, you chaps!' Mister Lewis shouted, waving his hat as he wafted after them.

Howling like sick wolves, Crunch and Wedge were racing across the bridge.

Mister Lewis stopped and wafted back to us, most of his head in place again, except for an ear and an eyebrow.

'Not using your head was a mighty stroke, Mister Lewis. How did you do that?' I asked.

'Do what, Milo?' he asked.

'Your head,' laughed Shane. 'Half of it was missing.'

'Oh dear, my head,' sighed Mister Lewis. 'Not again! Last time that happened was years ago when I first moved into the castle in town.'

'What's that got to do with losing heads?' I asked.

'Oh,' Mister Lewis sighed again. 'It's a well known fact that moving house is one of the most stressful things in one's life. And here I am about to move into a derelict old mill. And,' he went on, 'the bees, I was sorry about the bees. I just wanted to apologise to those young boys.'

'You *what*?' we both cried out.

'But … but they're the ones who snatched the bag,' I reminded him.

'I know,' Mister Lewis sighed again.

'And why did you disappear, anyway?'

Shane asked. 'We thought you'd done a runner on us.'

'I'd never do anything like that to my best friends,' Mister Lewis said. 'I disappeared when we saw people on the boat and then I simply decided that I should come together very slowly so that those boys wouldn't be scared.'

Shane and I hooted with laughter so much that I thought Shane would choke as he rolled around on the grass.

'Why is that funny?' Mister Lewis muttered with a scowl.

'Think about it, Mister Lewis,' I said, wiping my eyes. 'How would you feel if you were a kid and you saw boots and legs and skinny hands crawling out of a supermarket trolley?'

Mister Lewis's frown went as he finally got the picture. 'Oops,' he quipped, 'just as well I didn't catch up with them, eh?'

CHAPTER SIX

UP THE EERIE STAIRS

There was a KEEP OUT sign hanging sideways on the half-open door of the mill. Inside, it was eerily dark in some places and, apart from pigeons giving the odd warble above our heads, it was silent. The sort of worrying silence like when the principal stomps into the classroom to find out who has drawn the mad, crossed eyes on her photo in the entrance hall, and you're so scared that you almost put your hand up, even though you didn't do it.

'Hmm,' Mister Lewis mused as he looked around the dreary emptiness in the mill. 'This place didn't last long.'

'What do you mean?' I asked.

'Well,' he went on. 'When I was a lad there was a dilapidated house right here in this field. Rumour was that it was haunted, so nobody came here – people were more superstitious back in those days. Then, shortly before my unfortunate demise, work began on building a mill, using the stones from the knocked house. I didn't get to see it, of course,' he sighed and then paused. 'But the good part is that I got to have the best friends ever,' he said, grinning with his yellow teeth.

'Who were they?' began Shane.

'Us!' I said. 'Me and you, Shane.'

'Oh yeah,' he laughed.

Mister Lewis looked around at the patchy walls and the dirty floor. 'I think I should like to live upstairs,' he said. Which meant me and Shane puffing and panting as we pushed and pulled the trolley up the winding, rickety stairs.

When we reached the first landing, there was a loud cackle of hideous screeching. I ducked under the trolley and Shane curled up on the step, his hands over his head and his big bum in the air.

'It's all right,' Mister Lewis laughed. 'It's just a couple of crows.'

Sure enough, when I looked up through the skeletal rafters and some missing slates, I saw two screeching crows flapping about like plastic bags in the wind. 'I knew that,' I fibbed. 'I was just checking the wheels of the trolley.'

'Of course you were, Milo,' winked Mister Lewis.

'They look like witches,' put in Shane, still gaping upwards.

'You have too much imagination, Shane,' I muttered. 'They're just croaky old crows.'

When we finally got to the top of the stairs, we discovered two doors – but they were locked.

'There's probably just old machinery stuff in there, Mister Lewis,' said Shane. 'Don't worry, we'll find somewhere for your old bones.'

But Mister Lewis was totally fed up by now. 'It's no use, boys,' he sighed.

Then I noticed there was a third door around the corner, and this one was slightly open.

'There's an unlocked one here,' I called out, and politely stood back to let Mister

Lewis go in first.

'*Bawk, bawk*, chicken,' Shane muttered in my ear. 'Scaredy cat ...'

'I was just being mannerly,' I interrupted, hoping my ears wouldn't light up with the fib. Like Dad says, you'll always know a liar when the blood surges into his ears while he's being questioned in court.

'Ah, this will do nicely,' Mister Lewis was saying as we followed him in.

There was a musty smell – just like my damp football gear when it's left in the bag over the Easter holidays – but Mister Lewis said the smell didn't matter because his nose wasn't up to much anyway. Other than that, the floor was fairly clean and the windows were intact. There was even a small fireplace.

'This is grand,' said Mister Lewis. 'It must have been the watchman's place. See,' he went on, his eyes shining with delight, 'I'm

43

not going to be a derelict down-and-out spook looking longingly through windows or sheltering from the wind behind tombstones. I have a ROOM!'

We helped him to do a bit of cleaning and put his cushions on the floor. I placed his cat statue on the window ledge. After half an hour, the room seemed almost cosy.

'Well,' said Shane. 'That was a good day's work—' He didn't get any further because a loud, creepy droning sound prompted the two of us to back away towards the door, clinging to each other.

'Ah!' said Mister Lewis, waving his gloved hands and running to open the window. 'It's my bees! I told them where to come. Wait, boys, and say hello to my sweet beauties.'

But we were already halfway down the stairs. I mean, it was OK when they lived high up in the tower, but a cloud of stinging bees buzzing all over a small room is a definite reason to run.

★

Later that night, just as I was sinking into a dream about screaming horses, giant bees and claustrophobic baths, there was a tap-tapping at my window. At first, I thought it was part of my weird nightmare, but when I saw Mister Lewis's crooked hat and white face, I knew it was for real.

'Mister Lewis,' I said as I opened the window, 'what are you—?'

'Milo,' he panted, clutching my arm, 'it's the mill – it's haunted!'

CHAPTER SEVEN

MISS LEE IS ANNOYED

Mum was busy when I went down for breakfast the next morning. She had already punched up the cushions on the bamboo chairs in the sunroom, and now she was washing the china cups that she only uses for special occasions and when Dad's mum visits.

'What's happening, Mum?' I asked.

'It's my turn for the neighbourhood

ladies' afternoon tea,' she said with the sort of grim sigh that told me I should make myself scarce. Mum doesn't do fancy buns and cakes. She says there's no point in putting bakeries out of business. But she always feels that she has to make the effort for the neighbours because they'd suss out the shop stuff. Dad usually stays late in the Garda station on those days.

I called in for Shane on the way to school and told him about Mister Lewis's big scare.

'That's pure daft,' said Shane. 'How could one ghost scare another ghost?'

'Well,' I said, 'if you think about it, there are probably decent ghosts and bullying ghosts – just like there are good guys like you and me, and thugs like ...'

'Wedge and Crunch,' put in Shane. 'Yeah, that sounds kinda right. So where is Mister Lewis now?'

'In my wardrobe,' I sighed.

'Your wardrobe!' Shane spluttered. 'Why does he need to hide in a wardrobe when he can go invisible?'

'Well,' I began, 'when he's really stressed he has terrible nightmares and he tends to become visible. We just couldn't take that risk.'

'Huh?' Shane stopped and stared at me wide-eyed. 'Are you mad?' he screeched. 'What if your mum—?'

'That's the whole point,' I said. 'She doesn't venture into my bedroom. She says that she'd collapse into a coma if she went there, so I have to put my own stuff in the washing basket. And that suits me fine.'

Then I had a brilliant moment. 'Hey, Shane,' I said. 'Mum has some women neighbours coming to our house later on.'

'I know,' Shane put in. 'Gran is bringing

one of her African cakes.'

Shane's gran, Big Ella, makes the most awesome cakes ever. Now Mum would have something good to serve up instead of her crooked tarts and flat buns.

'While they're all chattering, Shane,' I said, 'you can come up to my room and say hello to Mister Lewis.'

'Sure thing,' laughed Shane as we made our way down to our classroom.

After eleven o'clock break Miss Lee lets us ask questions about stuff that's not on the school curriculum, because she says that it's sometimes good to talk outside the school books.

'What was it like in the war, Miss?' asked Willie Jones, the first to shoot his hand up. 'Me and my dad watched a film about it on telly. There was a woman in it and Dad said she was just like you, Miss.'

'Which war, Willie?' Miss Lee asked, with a puzzled frown.

'The big one, Miss,' Willie went on. 'The one with Hitler. What did you do when the bombs dropped, Miss?'

'Willie,' Miss Lee said calmly. 'When was that war?'

'Dunno, Miss.'

'It started in 1939,' Miss Lee said slowly. 'And it finished in 1945, Willie. How old do you think I am?'

Willie thought for a while, his face blank.

'I'm twenty-eight,' she went on. 'Now, do the maths, Willie.'

Willie screwed up his eyes as he tried to work out the sums, but the lights in his head were switched off. 'Dunno, Miss,' he said after a few seconds. 'So,' he continued, 'go on with the war, Miss. What was it like to be in it?'

We all laughed, especially Miss Lee.

After we settled down, Shane put up his hand. I bit my lip in fear that the question he'd cough up might make everyone holler again.

'Miss,' he began. 'Do you know that old mill near the river?'

'I do indeed know it, Shane,' she said.

Good thinking, I thought, giving him an approving nod.

'Could you tell us a bit about it?' Shane continued. 'You know everything about the history of the town,' he added, just to get on her good side.

There were groans of 'boring' and 'poncy' from some of the hard guys. Miss Lee quietened them when she suggested switching to sums. There was a hush and we all sighed when she began. Not that the class were interested; it was the dossing that delighted most of them.

Miss Lee cleared her throat. 'All that land around the mill was owned by the rich Maguire clan, who lived there in a fine house from the sixteen hundreds until the eighteen sixties.' She went on. 'They even had their own burial place in a mausoleum they had built on their land—'

'Us too!' interrupted Willie Jones. 'We bury all our cats on our land.'

'I hope they're dead,' someone from the back shouted.

Even Miss Lee laughed at that.

'Go on with the story, Miss,' said Shane. 'Tell us about the mill.'

'Indeed,' said Miss Lee. 'I'm coming to that, Shane. Well, the last of the family was a reclusive old man, Niall Maguire—'

Another hand went up. 'What does reclusive mean, Miss?'

Miss Lee gave a big sigh. 'It means that

he didn't mix with people. Apart from a delivery boy who brought him his groceries from the town, nobody was welcomed into the big, rambling house, which gradually began to deteriorate with dampness and crumbling plaster. When he died, Niall was buried with his ancestors.'

'What happened the house, Miss?' I asked.

'A distant cousin from Kildare took over,' she said. 'His name was Timothy McDonnell Maguire.'

'That's two surnames, Miss,' someone interrupted. 'That's real posh.'

Miss Lee nodded. 'Some people still like to keep family names from the mother's side,' she explained.

'Well,' said Tim McCarthy, the guy who sits near me, 'if people still used two surnames, I would be Timothy Harty McCarthy.'

'Indeed,' Miss Lee sighed.

Quick as a flash, Willie Jones called out that Tim could even have THREE surnames. 'That'd be well posh,' he added.

Tim grinned with pride. 'Really?' he said. 'Cool.'

Guessing exactly where Willie was going with rhyming names, Miss Lee said sharply, 'That's enough for now. Get out your maths workbooks.'

We all glared at Willie.

'But, Miss,' Shane wailed. 'What about the mill?'

'Yes, go on, Miss,' I added in support.

'That can wait for another time,' she said, 'when we can have a mature conversation.'

CHAPTER EIGHT

THE BEES

After school, Shane and me were heading home when we spotted Crunch coming out of the supermarket with his mum. His nose was still dotted with green cream. He scowled at us when Shane said hello and asked him sweetly how he was feeling. What was Shane thinking, being all sweet and jolly to our enemy? Of course I had to wade in too. 'Tough luck,' I muttered. 'Poor nose.'

'None of your business,' he snarled.

His mum gave him a whack on the ear. 'You talk good to those nice boys,' she said.

'It's OK, Missus,' said Shane. 'We understand. A bee sting is pretty painful.'

'And two or more are totally painful,' I added, trying to sound sympathetic.

'So mind yourself, Crunch,' said Shane. 'Bees are dangerous.'

'Deadly dangerous,' I added, hoping that would make him think twice before trying to tackle us again.

Even under the green cream, we could see Crunch's mouth silently muttering stronger words.

His mum saw it too. 'You say goodbye,' she said, giving her son another dig. 'We need to get you home. You don't want to be late for the bus.'

'You going somewhere, Crunch?' I asked.

But his mum was pulling him along the street.

'That felt good,' laughed Shane as we moved along.

Until next time we see him, I thought. Maybe we should have said nothing. Still, his mum was a feisty lady who liked good manners, so she might be on our side.

When we let ourselves into my house, we gagged at the smell of Mum's fancy candles in the hall. There was loud chatter and laughter from the sunroom.

'Mum! Me and Shane are just going up to my room,' I called out from the hall and hoped she wouldn't haul us in to be exhibited to the women.

'To do some work, Missus Doyle,' Shane fibbed, giving me a wink. 'Hard sums,' he added.

'Good. You are such diligent boys,' Mum

said, loud enough for all to hear.

'Yes, we are,' replied Shane in his oiliest good-guy voice. 'What does "diligent" mean, Milo?' he whispered as we went upstairs.

'Dunno,' I sniggered. 'But it must be harmless.'

My grin faded when we got to my room and I looked at the wardrobe. The door was wide open and so was my window. 'He's not here!' I exclaimed. 'Mister Lewis is not here! He must have gone back to the mill.'

'Oh shoot!' wailed Shane. 'You said he'd help us find out about the mill and stuff.'

'Well, how was I to know he'd skive off...' I began. Then, as I looked around, my heart jumped, like, all the way up to my head.

'My telly!' I cried. 'Someone has broken in and nicked my telly and scared Mister Lewis away!'

'No way,' said Shane, rushing over to examine the table where I keep my telly – as if it would pop up by itself and say boo!

'Hellooo,' said a sleepy voice from under my bed.

'Mister Lewis!' I laughed with relief. 'Why are you under there?'

'Eh, for comfort, lad, and to stay hidden – just in case your mum might look in and see me with this TV gadget that I've seen you play with. But no matter how much I press buttons or shake it, nothing happens, so I had a good sleep instead.'

'Wow!' laughed Shane, peering under the other side of the bed. 'He's even tried your XBox, Milo. But he hasn't plugged anything in!'

'Ah, so that's where I went wrong,' said Mister Lewis. 'I thought it might be fun,' he went on as he stood up and stretched his skinny arms. 'It gets boring when you're not here, Milo. I've read most of your books, especially *Skulduggery Pleasant* and *Extreme Adventures*. I've even been back to the museum, but there's no fun in scaring the same people all the time.'

Then he gave a great sigh. 'I feel I should put on a brave face and venture back to the mill and try to be a proper ghost ...' He stopped when we heard a loud, screechy commotion from downstairs.

Mister Lewis clapped his hands to his ears. 'The women! It's those awful women! Oh lawks!'

'Mister Lewis!' I said valiantly. 'Don't talk about my mum and her friends like that.'

'Nor my gran,' put in Shane.

'No, no, boys! It's those scary women from the mill. I could hear them at night, shrieking in the other rooms ...'

'The ones you told me about last night?'
I asked, but Mister Lewis was already going
invisible.

We ran down the stairs towards the ear-
splitting screams of Mum and her guests
as they scrambled towards the front door,
frantically waving their hands over their
heads.

'Mum!' I cried.

She turned and waved me away. 'Run
back to your room, Milo, and close the door
tight. Go NOW!' she added, just before
running outside and slamming the door.

'Come this way, lads,' said Mister Lewis,
becoming visible again and heading towards
the sunroom, which was in a right old mess
with half-eaten cakes and tarts scattered
over the floor. The good china cups were
in bits. But it was the creepy droning sound
that brought us to a standstill. The big, open

windows were alive with bees that just kept on coming through.

'Ah, it's my little darlings,' Mister Lewis sighed with relief. 'Come to Papa,' he whispered, extending his two skinny arms. I shuddered when I saw the bees settle on his hands, arms and shoulders.

'I figured you might have had something to do with this, Mister Lewis,' a voice chuckled from one of the armchairs.

'Gran!' Shane yelled. 'Run! Save yourself from those bees!'

'Bees?' she said, getting up from the chair. 'No, my love. These dozy little dots of yellow and black are all noise and nonsense. Now, if this was Africa where real bees are big, loud and mean, we'd be lying on the floor, screaming.' Then she put out her hands and more bees flew to her.

'My dear lady!' exclaimed Mister Lewis.

'As usual you utterly amaze me.'

'I think we ought to move,' said Big Ella. 'Let's get these poor things to a safe place before those hysterical ladies send for someone to get rid of them.'

'My mum wouldn't ...' I began loyally. But when I thought it through, I figured that was exactly what Mum would do. I've seen her jump on spiders.

Mister Lewis took off his hat and held it out. 'Come along, my sweet friends,' he said over the continuous hum. Within seconds, the bees came together, as if by magic, and swarmed into the hat. 'Quiet now,' he whispered to them. 'Time for us to go home.'

'Can you go invisible, Mister Lewis?' I asked, thinking of the commotion outside.

He shook his head. 'No, Milo,' he said. 'Not while I'm carrying a hatful of bees.'

'Oh shoot!' said Shane. 'What'll we do?'

'We'll stay calm, that's what we'll do,' said Big Ella. 'Mister Lewis,' she went on, 'you go out the back door with the bees and make your way along the lane to my back garden. The key is under a flowerpot at the back door. Myself and the boys will go outside and tell the ladies that the bees have left and that all is well.'

CHAPTER NINE

HELP FROM BIG ELLA

'Big Ella! Milo! Shane!' Mum screeched when the three of us came out of the house. 'You should have stayed safe in your room, Milo. You too, Big Ella,' she added. 'I thought you were with us. Were you stung?'

'The bees have left, my dear,' said Big Ella. 'Everything is OK.'

'Big Ella, how did you manage?' began Mrs Grace.

'Oh, I'm used to giant bees in Africa,' Big Ella laughed. 'One learns how to deal with them and send them on their way home.'

There was much oooing and aaahhing from the women as they patted Big Ella and said what a brave lady she was.

'I'll take the boys to my house for tea whilst you ladies clean up the mess,' said Big Ella.

How cool was that!

When we arrived, Mister Lewis was sitting in her kitchen, talking gently to the hatful of bees on his lap.

'My clever friends,' he said.

'Oh, it was nothing, Mister Lewis,' said Shane. 'Me and Milo can handle anything ...'

'I think Mister Lewis is talking about his bees, Shane,' chuckled Big Ella. 'Now let's pack some buns and get him and his bees back to their new home. Shane tells me that it's an old mill, Mister Lewis. How quaint.'

Mister Lewis's waxy face went a paler shade of its usual porridge colour as he munched a bun.

'I think not, Big Ella,' he sighed. 'Those women ...'

'Women?' said Big Ella.

'In the mill, Gran,' put in Shane. 'Mister Lewis says they're there, but me and Milo didn't see or hear them.'

'All we heard was squawking crows,' I said. 'Women can sound like that ...' I tapered off when Big Ella laughed.

Mister Lewis was shaking his head – obviously a bit confused between crows and women.

'Well then,' said Big Ella, picking up her big bag. 'Let's go and sort this out. No buts,' she went on when Mister Lewis got a bit agitated. 'You must be brave, Mister Lewis. When I lived in deepest Africa there were some spooky characters who *thought* they were from the netherworld and frightened many decent folks. But people like me stood up to them and they'd usually go away.'

'Usually?' Mister Lewis said, with a tremor in his voice.

'Ah, except for the real ones who'd bite heads off,' said Big Ella. She laughed when Mister Lewis's face turned green.

'I'm joking,' she said. 'There's no such thing as ghosts ...' Then her voice tapered off. 'Oops. Sorry!' she whispered.

'Ghosts?' laughed Mister Lewis. 'I think you'll find, dear lady, that there are more displaced ghosts like me out there. And that's what bothers me.'

CHAPTER TEN

WHO TRASHED THE ROOM?

Big Ella's car coughed into life after several turns of the key; each time it died, Mister Lewis almost did the same – died again, I mean.

'I've never been in one of these contraptions,' he said, clutching his hatful of bees.

Truth is, it *was* a contraption that Big

69

Ella had bought from a man who'd left the country – that's what my dad told me. Something to do with a banjaxed heist of farm chickens whose owner had a fine swing with a hurley.

Another splutter and the car moved, and so did Mister Lewis, wafting behind the back seat with his precious hatful of bees that were buzzing drowsily.

'Oh, what a lovely view,' exclaimed Big Ella when we crossed the bridge. The car screeched to a halt at the wall that overlooked the field and the old mill.

'This is just perfect for you, Mister Lewis,' she said as she locked the car. 'So much nicer than the dusty tower. And look, there are lots of flowers with healthy pollen for your bees,' she gushed.

We walked along the track towards the mill, keeping a good distance from the horses' field. Not that *that* made any difference. When Mister Lewis caught up with us, after rounding up a few stray bees, the horses went mental again.

'Goodness,' said Big Ella. 'Such noisy creatures!'

Me and Shane glanced at each other, but neither of us would spill the beans that it was Mister Lewis who was responsible for the horses' behaviour.

Big Ella admired the run-down mill and said it must have been beautiful in olden times. And she didn't mind puffing up the winding stairs. But when we passed the two locked doors she gave a sort of shiver.

'Are you cold, Big Ella?' asked Mister Lewis when he reached his own door.

'Oh, not at all,' she replied. 'Just a slight draught. You folks must have felt it too ...'

She broke off when Mister Lewis opened

his door and let out a shrill cry. 'My goodness!' he exclaimed. 'Look at this mess!'

Well, there certainly was a mess: the cushions had been thrown around, eggs were broken on the floor and all our tidying had been undone.

'Who would do something like this?' wondered Big Ella, her hands on her hips and her face scrunched with anger. 'Don't tell me,' she went on. 'It could only be those two whatsernames, Podge and Munch.'

'I hope so,' sighed Mister Lewis.

'What do you mean?' I asked. 'Why would you want them to do this?'

'Because they're ordinary living humans,' he said, 'and I can deal with them. But …' His voice tapered off.

'Are you back to thinking about those scary dead folks, Mister Lewis?' muttered Big Ella. 'You settle down, honey. This is the work of a couple of no-good youngsters. Now let's get to work.'

We cleaned up as best we could and left the place a bit more comfortable.

'Just you remember, Mister Lewis,' said Big Ella as we were leaving, 'I'll give those boys a right earful for what they've done and they'll never do anything like this again, believe me.'

'I do hope you're right, Big Ella,' sighed Mister Lewis.

CHAPTER ELEVEN

MISS LEE'S STORY

Next morning, which was Saturday, I called in to Shane's house. Big Ella drove us into town and dropped us off near the castle because she was going shopping and said that if Shane was with her he'd fill the trolley with junk. We spotted Miss Lee going through the castle gates – she's friendly with some of the staff in there – so we sauntered in to see what was happening with Mister Lewis's tower.

The broken door was in a big skip along with other old bits, including a grotty blanket that Mister Lewis had left behind in his hurry to get away. That made me sort of sentimental for a few seconds. We could see that the rickety stairs were also gone. In their place were brand-new stairs with a polished, snake-like banister that curved around the cleaned stones of the wall. We stood back to look up at the slotted windows above.

'It's looking good already, Milo,' Shane whispered. Then he gave a great sigh. 'Still and all, I liked it most when Mister Lewis was there.'

'Me too,' I said. 'I wonder will he ever get to come back here.'

'Nah,' Shane sighed. 'It'll be all shiny and posh and full of history nerds who will be up and down the new stairs, so he'd have to spend all his time hiding or going invisible a lot.'

'Hoi!' A man wearing a yellow helmet leaned out from a high window. 'Hoppit, you two. You're trespassing.'

'We're just having a look,' Shane called back. 'Our friend lived up there.'

'Yeah, right,' the man shouted. 'What century was that? Take yourselves and your imaginary friend out of here. This place is out of bounds.'

Before Shane could think up some more cheeky words, we heard the familiar clip-clop of Miss Lee's high heels crossing the courtyard. As usual, she was carrying a couple of books.

'Milo, Shane,' she said. 'What are you two doing here?'

'Just looking, Miss,' I said.

'Yeah,' added Shane. 'We have cool memories of the old tower.'

Which I thought was a very nice answer.

'Me too, Shane,' replied our teacher. 'But wait until you see it when it's done up. It will be superb. By the way,' she went on, 'I was sorry I didn't get to your questions yesterday.'

'About the mill?' I asked. 'Can you tell us a bit more now?'

We both held our breath while she looked at her watch.

'Umm,' she began. 'I have some time to kill. Well, since you're both so eager, let's go and have tea and buns in the Hungry Duck.'

'Sure thing, Miss Lee,' whooped Shane, rubbing his tummy in anticipation as we headed down the street.

'So, the old mill,' Miss Lee began when

we sat at a table and ordered hot chocolate and buns. 'What do you want to know?'

'Everything,' said Shane. 'After when you threw that wobbly at school— Ouch!' he yelped when I kicked his ankle.

Miss Lee laughed. 'Sometimes a teacher is entitled to throw a wobbly,' she said. 'Otherwise we'd explode. Now, let's focus on what you want to know.'

'The mill,' I said.

'All right,' she began. 'You probably don't know this, but that mill never actually functioned.'

'What does that mean?' asked Shane.

'It means that it was never finished, never actually worked.'

'Why not?' I asked.

'Because,' Miss Lee went on, 'it was said to have been haunted for very many years. Listen now and I'll tell you from where we left off yesterday.'

So she told us that when the old man who was the last of the Maguire clan died in the eighteen sixties, a distant relative, Timothy McDonnell Maguire, took over. He wasn't interested in restoring the old Maguire mansion. All he wanted was the land, so he set about knocking down the house so that he could use the stones to build a mill. Mills were very important back then,' she said.

'So where did he stay and eat after he knocked down the house?' asked Shane.

Me and Miss Lee laughed. 'Trust you to be concerned about food and comfort, Shane,' she said. 'There would have been a hostelry, a sort of old-fashioned hotel, in the town back then.'

'Go on about the stones, Miss,' I said before Shane could ask about what sort of grub there would have been in the hostelry.

'Yes, the stones,' Miss Lee continued. 'Well, when he ran out of stones, he actually tore down the whole family mausoleum.'

'A mousy what, Miss?' asked Shane.

'It's a private burial house for very rich people who like to be buried on their own land,' said Miss Lee. 'Using those stones to build the mill was not a clever move. After that, scary things began to happen. The local men who were building the mill saw weird figures that flitted scarily about the building works. Anyway, it got so bad that the workers left – even though the money was good.'

'What did McDonnell Maguire do then?' I asked.

'That's the strange thing,' Miss Lee said in a whisper. 'One morning his body was found beside the makeshift grave he'd dug to bury the skeletal remains from the mausoleum.

There were no marks on his body, no blood anywhere. The local doctor, whose notes are in the town library, couldn't find anything wrong with the body.'

'That's very interesting, Miss,' said Shane.

'Well, thank you, Shane.'

'Miss, would you bring us to see a mau—, a mousey—, a boney place sometime, Miss? That'd be great crack.'

CHAPTER TWELVE

LOOKING FOR MISTER LEWIS

'That was totally scary, Milo,' Shane said as we went through town.

I nodded, still thinking over Miss Lee's words.

'Do you believe all that?' Shane asked. 'About the mill?'

'I don't want to believe it, Shane,' I said. 'But Miss Lee wouldn't tell us a fib. And she did say that there hasn't been any weird stuff there for ages, but people don't tend to go there because of the stories they'd have heard for years and years.'

'Imagine that guy — what's his name?' began Shane.

'McDonnell Maguire,' I said.

'Yeah, him. Imagine knocking down the dead people's place ...'

'You mean the mausoleum,' I interrupted, because I like to flash new words before I forget them.

'That's right,' Shane went on. 'No wonder weird things started happening. You can't go messing with dead people.'

It scared me to think of Mister Lewis alone in that mill.

'Do you think the Maguires might come after Mister Lewis, Milo? We can't leave him there on his own,' Shane went on. 'He's a good friend and he must be scared stiff. He might even be dead!'

'Shane, he's already dead,' I said. 'Been dead for over a hundred years.'

'Oh yeah,' sighed Shane. 'But in our minds, he'll always be our spooky pal.'

Well, his words were very poetic and something sparked in my head. 'Right,' I said before I could change my mind. 'Let's go to the mill.'

'Serious?' Shane's voice wobbled.

'Positively serious,' I said. 'Could we ever live with ourselves if we didn't at least check the place?'

'You're right,' Shane sighed. 'Let's do it.'

So we went the same route – was it only recently we'd helped Mister Lewis with his pathetic few things in a supermarket trolley?

As we walked warily through the field towards the mill, I so wished we were simply going to have fun and chat with the old guy, instead of worrying about whether he'd be all scattered bones and rags – that was the image that kept coming into my mind. I didn't mention that to Shane because he'd freak out. But he had already tuned in to my mind, though not in a nice way.

'Milo,' he whispered, 'what'll we do if we find bits of Mister Lewis all over the place? What part of him would you take to remember him by?'

'Huh? That's gross!' I hollered. 'You're a sicko.'

'No, I'm not,' he retorted. 'Gran told me that years ago when she was young, people used to keep small bones of dead folks and talk to them – the bones, I mean.'

'That's double gross,' I snapped and put my hands over my ears. Like I needed that sort of talk when we were hoping to see our dead friend alive. Well, you know what I mean.

The door of the mill was open.

'It's quiet,' I said, as we tip-toed warily up the winding stairs.

'What did you expect?' asked Shane. 'Trumpets and drums, huh?'

He was still miffed with me over the bones thing.

The first thing we saw when we went in through the half-open door was Mister Lewis's hat. But, yet again, no Mister Lewis.

CHAPTER THIRTEEN

MILO'S PLAN

Neither of us said anything – it was like we were waiting for him to waft along and be glad to see us. The room was pretty messy, which was strange because Mister Lewis is what Big Ella calls a 'real tidy gentleman'.

'What will we do, Milo?' whispered Shane, staying close beside me.

'Dunno,' I gulped, picking up the hat.

We stood nervously together, looking around the room.

'What's going on, Milo?' whispered Shane. 'Mister Lewis wouldn't go anywhere without his hat.'

Then we heard a shuffly groaning sound from behind an upturned armchair, and we both made a dash for the door, me still clutching Shane's jacket and him hanging on to my Man U sweatshirt.

'It's me, boys! And I'm so very glad to see you.'

We turned to see Mister Lewis's body becoming visible from behind the chair. I've always wished he wouldn't do that. It freaks me out.

'Whoo,' gasped Shane. 'Are we glad to see you!'

'Not half as much as I am to see you two,' Mister Lewis sighed.

'What's going on, Mister Lewis?' I asked as I handed him his hat.

He sighed again as he wiped the hat with his gloved hand. 'It's those women from next door,' he said. 'They're witches!'

'Witches?' Shane and I said together.

'Witches are just fairytale folks, Mister Lewis,' I said as calmly as I could.

'Were they wearing pointy hats?' asked Shane.

'No,' Mister Lewis replied.

'What about big noses and hairy chins?' I put in.

Mister Lewis shook his head.

'What about broomsticks?' Shane asked.

'No, nothing like that,' sighed Mister Lewis. 'They just barged in and snatched the buns that Big Ella gave me!'

'Well then,' said Shane, 'they're definitely not witches.'

'It's true, Mister Lewis,' I added. 'My dad is a Garda and he says times are so bad that there are people who can't pay rent so they get turfed out of their homes and try to find shelter anywhere.'

'Especially derelict buildings like this,' put in Shane.

Mister Lewis sighed again. 'Well, whoever they are, look what they've done to my lovely room. They just barged in without knocking and went around messing with my things. I can't stay here with shrieking crones like them. Where shall I go now? I'm tired of moving about.'

I looked at him, with his crooked hat and wobbly nose and it was like a big surge of electricity went through me from my toes right up to my head.

'Listen, Mister Lewis,' I said. 'Me and Shane will help you.'

Shane's eyebrows shot up his forehead. 'What?' he said.

'We're not afraid of a couple of straggly women with no manners,' I nodded to him.

'Sure,' said Shane. 'We'll ... we'll ...'

'We'll work something out,' I put in. 'Now let's clean up here and we'll be back later.'

'Huh?' said Shane, sounding like he wanted to object – until he saw my frown. 'Er, yeah,' he went on. If they come sniffing around, you tell them that you have tough guys coming who'll sort them out.'

It was good to see Mister Lewis smiling again, even if there was still fear in his eyes.

'Thank you, boys,' he said. 'You have cheered me up already. With your help, we'll handle this together. I'm staying put,' he added decisively.

Fighting words, but we both knew that he was mad scared. And so were we.

'What were you thinking, Milo?' asked Shane shortly afterwards as we headed for home. 'How are we supposed to deal with a couple of wild women with no manners?'

'I know,' I said. 'But I felt so sorry for him. I just wanted—'

'I wonder where the horses are,' Shane interrupted. 'There's still no sign of them. Come on, let's see where they are. It'll give us a bit of reality after Mister Lewis's stuff,' he went on as he ran towards the field.

I sighed as I followed. Much as I like horses, I just wanted to get away from here, and I wondered how we could possibly help Mister Lewis against two wild women.

Up ahead, Shane stood on a bar of the gate.

'Milo!' he shouted. 'All the horses are gone. The whole field is empty.'

'Maybe they've just been moved to a different field,' I called out.

'No way!' Shane shouted back. 'The far

gate is broken in bits. It's like they barged right through it.'

'Crunch and Wedge!' we both said together.

'Imagine those two getting their evil fun by chasing poor horses around the field and making them break through that gate,' said Shane.

'Creeps, the pair of them,' I said angrily.

CHAPTER FOURTEEN

SLEEPOVER

Mum was taking a shepherd's pie out of the microwave when I got home at teatime. I hoped it was the last one. Mum feels that she's being really clever by making a load of pies at the same time and then freezing them. She says it makes life easier – though, frankly I prefer Dad's idea of cooking, when Mum is out with friends and he phones for a delivery of fish and chips and we watch telly. I sneaked upstairs before she saw my muddy shoes and dirty hands.

'Come on, Milo,' she called up after a few minutes. 'We can't wait for your dad.' (She always puts in the *your dad* bit when she's annoyed with him.)

'Any news, Milo?' she asked when I sat down at the table.

The real answer went whirling inside my head. *Yes, Mum. Me and Shane are going to spend the night saving a dead man from a couple of loco women who are driving him mad.*

'Nothing much, Mum,' I said. 'Me and Shane had a chat with Miss Lee about history stuff.'

'Good lads,' she nodded as she dished out the shepherd's pie. 'You two will go far.'

Well, that was for sure, I thought, considering my promise to Mister Lewis. 'Going far' might be somewhere up there on a cold moon with raggedy corpses floating about on it. But then I shook my head to stop crazy thoughts; after all, in spite of Mister Lewis's weird imagination, a couple of poor women could be tamed.

Halfway through our meal, Dad came in. He was sweating and his shoes were even muddier than mine.

'Heavens, man,' Mum exclaimed. 'Where have you been? Look at the state of you.'

'We were out looking for Harry Donnelly's horses,' Dad said. 'They were all over the place ... Oh, shepherd's pie again,' he said as he dried his hands. 'Lovely.'

'Did you find them, Dad?' I asked. 'The horses.'

'We did – eventually,' he said, shaking lots of pepper on his dinner. 'They broke into a couple of farms. Very strange,' he went on. 'Every one of them was shivering. They were really scared.'

'What scared them?' Mum asked. 'Perhaps a couple of youngsters messing about in the night?'

'No,' said Dad. 'I've never seen anything like it. Those horses were extremely traumatised – as if the devil himself was after them. We had to put them into another farmer's field because they refused to go back along the road to Harry's. I've never heard such a commotion.'

'Is it OK if I stay with Shane tonight?' I cleverly asked while they were absorbed in the runaway horses.

'Sure,' said Mum. 'That means we can watch what we like on telly.'

I rushed upstairs and packed two torches, matches and a couple of candles.

'Have a good time, and be good,' Mum called out as I ran down the stairs.

'And stay alive,' I muttered to myself,

trying not to think of what might happen in a dreary old mill with just a dead man for company.

I called in for Shane, who had already told Big Ella that he'd be sleeping in my house.

'And please don't phone me, Gran,' he said, putting his bag over his shoulder. 'And don't phone Milo's mum because I'm not a baby. OK?'

'OK,' laughed Big Ella. 'Here.' She went to the fridge and took out a box of goodies. 'I know you boys,' she laughed, handing it to Shane. 'You'll probably be peckish at midnight.'

'Oh, we'll have a blast, Gran,' Shane replied.

'Well, have a good time now,' she smiled.

'I wish,' I whispered.

'We'll be fine, Milo,' said Shane, closing the front door. 'And look,' he went on as he fished something from his pocket. 'I've brought my mouth organ to help while away the time.'

'Or we could just play I Spy,' I said, because I know how he plays the mouth organ and I felt a headache forming already.

'No, this will keep us calm during the night, Milo,' he said seriously.

I took a deep breath and hoped he might lose it on the way.

Naturally we brought our schoolbags with us — it would be pretty awkward if we'd left them behind and Big Ella and my parents found them next morning!

On the way down Main Street we saw Jimmy Riley's bus pulling in and a gang of guys from fifth and sixth classes got out, all wearing football gear and chattering like high-pitched starlings. We were amazed to see Wedge and Crunch among them.

'Ha, look at Sleepy and Grumpy,' laughed

Wedge. 'We've been at a soccer blitz, while you two were mincing around the town like girls.'

'Our whole class was away since yesterday,' added Freddie Murphy.

'We were in a posh school with a big soccer pitch,' boasted Wedge. 'We had a blast. Soccer all yesterday evening and this morning. Pure cool! They even have lights.'

'Yeah,' put in Crunch, whose bee stings had settled down nicely. 'But not a place for losers like you nerds,' he added in a whisper.

'How come you got to go there?' asked Shane.

'The boarder guys were away on a break, and our teacher Mister Dunne is friendly with the principal,' said Crunch. 'That's how we got invited to play on the pitch yesterday and this morning.'

'And we got to stay the night,' Wedge gloated.

'In sleeping bags!' added Dave Malone. 'It was mega fun.'

That's when it hit me. 'Shane!' I hissed, dragging him away.

'What's wrong, Milo?' he asked.

'They've been away since yesterday! Remember Crunch's ma telling him not to miss the bus?'

'Yeah, so?' Shane put in impatiently.

'Think,' I said.

And then he got the message. 'Hey, Milo!' he exclaimed. 'That means it couldn't have been Wedge and Crunch who chased the horses.'

Well, if we were scared before, we were heart-thumpingly panicky now.

'What'll we do, Milo?' Shane asked in a low,

quiet voice to stop himself from screaming. 'Maybe leave it till tomorrow, huh?'

Several things shot through my mind – all of them cowardly. But I thought of Mister Lewis alone in that old mill with just a couple of loonies and his bees for company. We had made a promise. So there was no turning back from the scariest decision ever.

CHAPTER FIFTEEN

GATECRASHERS

'It's Milo and Shane!' we called out, so that Mister Lewis wouldn't be scared when he heard our voices.

'Come in, come in!' Mister Lewis whooped, looking over our shoulders to check that it was just us. 'I'm so glad you're here,' he sighed as he locked the door and pushed a rickety chair up against the handle.

Shane and I looked at each other with amazement – like this wood-wormy chair and rusty lock would keep out anyone that'd come knocking? No way. We'd already heard those croaky crow sounds above the rafters again and I wished the door was made of solid iron.

'I know what you chaps are thinking,' Mister Lewis said as we eased ourselves onto the cushions.

'You can read our minds?' Shane almost choked and he pulled his jacket over his head to hold in his thoughts.

'No, lad,' said Mister Lewis, shaking his head and wobbly nose. 'Indeed no. What I mean is that I imagine you're both wondering why I've decided to stay put in this place.'

'So why *are* you staying?' I had to ask. 'It's well creepy. You can still come back to my wardrobe.'

'I know that, Milo,' he whispered. 'But,

if you think about it, I'm pretty creepy too, so I decided that I wasn't going to be intimidated. It's time I stuck up for myself.'

'Good thinking, Mister Lewis,' said Shane, with over-the-top enthusiasm. 'We'll be right behind you, me and Milo.'

We chatted a bit about school, because that's the sort of stuff Mister Lewis likes to hear. He says that school in his time was all whacks and yells and freezing classrooms, and he never can understand how we could see 'moving pictures in a box'. The first time he saw Big Ella's telly, I switched it on to show him how it works. Unfortunately, it was an old Dracula film. He screamed all the way back to the tower – people talked about that sound for days afterwards.

It was beginning to get dark now, so we lit the candles and put them on the mantelpiece, leaving the torches until later to preserve the batteries. Shane freaked out when one of the candles cast his shadow on the wall and only settled down when we put out the goodies that Big Ella had given us for our fake 'sleepover'. The buns and cakes and fizzy coke took our minds off all things eerie. When the sky outside got darker, we lit the torches. We were actually so relaxed we were laughing at one of Mister Lewis's stories when suddenly the doorknob rattled. We froze, like glassy-eyed dummies in a shop window. I swallowed the sausage I'd been chewing and half wished I'd choke and pass out before whatever was out there would enter. There it was again, that rattle.

'Don't worry, boys,' whispered Mister Lewis. 'The door is locked.'

Like that was comforting? I was too numb to even yell when the door splintered.

Worse still, Mister Lewis wafted towards the door of his small bedroom farther across the room. He turned to Shane and me and put his finger to his dead white lips. 'Sshh,' he whispered before going through a wall, 'I'll be back.'

CHAPTER SIXTEEN

RAGGEDY HAGS

The awful shrieks of whoever was hammering the door made me want to leap through the window. Shane was holding my arm so tightly my fingers went numb. But my biggest scare was that there was no way to escape.

The door burst open and a raggedy woman barged in, causing the candles to splutter. She was tall and skinny with hair like mangy cats' tails under what looked like a battered pirate hat. Her black dress had lots of patches, which didn't quite cover some of the holes.

'Ah, food,' she cackled. 'Ooh, are those new breads? Come, Eulalia,' she bellowed, ignoring me and Shane, 'there are wondrous items to fill our bellies.'

Eulalia stepped over the broken chair, a wide, gappy grin on her face. She too was wearing a grotty black dress and pirate hat. Her eyes lit up when she spotted the food. 'Is it real, Mellie?' she whooped as she lunged across the room like a pin to a magnet.

Without so much as a *how do you do and may we join you?*, they launched into our precious food with their bare hands, stuffing Big Ella's sandwiches and buns into their wide mouths, slurping our coke and belching loudly.

Shane and myself stood like zombies, too

dumb to move. What was Mister Lewis thinking, leaving us on our own?

'Don't worry, Milo,' Shane whispered in my ear. 'Just remember that they're only poor, raggedy folks who've probably been put out of their home. Just like other down-and-outs. They'll go away when they've had a bit of food.'

But when they hurled themselves at Shane's favourite chocolate cake he went ballistic. If there's anything that fires Shane's temper, it's when anyone messes with Big Ella's special, scrumptious chocolate cake.

'Whoa!' he bellowed. 'You've scoffed enough already. That's my cake. Hands off!'

That's when Mister Lewis came back, this time through a door. He was holding a big umbrella with several spokes hanging loose.

Shane glanced at me and shook his head.

'Perhaps you ought to leave now, ladies,'

Mister Lewis said politely.

The 'ladies' looked up at us like a couple of hungry tigers spotting their prey for the first time.

'We are not going anywhere, old man,' snarled Eulalia through a big, slobbering mouthful of cake.

Mister Lewis's worried face was like dough that had been kneaded by dirty hands. 'As a gentleman I regret having to do this,' he said, reaching up to poke the beehive high up over the window with the bockety umbrella. The bees flew out onto the umbrella and Mister Lewis shook them loose. They knew exactly what to do, flying like war planes towards the enemy.

'Cool,' said Shane, nudging me in the ribs. 'That'll get rid of those two skinny mollies.'

We watched with glee as the bees circled over the cakes.

'Wait for it,' I whispered.

Wait nothing! The bees buzzed over them, took one look at the women and then zoomed straight back into the hive. If there had been a door on the hive, they would have slammed it.

Mister Lewis sighed deeply and shook his head. I mean, there's nothing you can do if your bees decide that home is best when there's trouble brewing. And I found myself wishing that we could do the same.

'Pardon me,' said Mister Lewis, but not as loud this time and with a note of defeat. 'I really do think you have perhaps had enough. My two young guests and myself are simply having a quiet evening, so if you wouldn't mind ...'

'We're not going anywhere, old man,' growled Mellie.

'No, indeed,' said her sister, wiping her

mouth with her sleeve. 'There's much food to consume. We haven't eaten for such a long, long while.'

'Huh, they're making up for it now,' muttered Shane.

'Excuse me.' Mister Lewis was beginning to sharpen his voice. 'I think you ought to go back to your own rooms.'

'Sit down, old man,' snarled Eulalia. 'We shall leave when our stomachs are replete. Our hunger is great.'

'We have not eaten such food for over four hundred years,' said the other, Mellie, through a mouthful of bun.

'Did she say four hundred years, Milo?' Shane whispered, pinching my arm.

I had no answer to that because my mouth had dried up with fear.

'Ah,' said Mister Lewis, politely. 'Like myself, you are halfway spirits too.'

For just a few seconds the two women stopped munching to stare at Mister Lewis.

'We don't know what you talk about, old man,' said Mellie. 'All of this land belongs to us since it was taken by our ancestor Granuaile.'

'We have got rid of everyone who tried to take it,' put in Eulalia. 'Some, perhaps, took longer than others, but we chased them all,' she added with a laugh.

'The last one being the foolish man who tried to build this mill,' Mellie sniggered.

'So,' put in her sister. 'You are not welcome here, old man. This is our watch, to keep safe the land of our ancestors.'

'Just great,' whispered Shane. 'Now we have three bloomin' ghosts. I don't like this, Milo,' he went on. 'I'd like to go home now.'

I looked at the two 'ladies', still stuffing food into their skinny faces, not having eaten for years and years. That's when I came up with my master stroke of genius. A lightbulb switched on inside my head.

CHAPTER SEVENTEEN

SHANE PLAYS A TUNE

'Shane,' I whispered. 'Get out your mouth organ.'

'Huh? Are you mad?' he hissed. 'This is not the time for music.'

'Just take it out and play it,' I went on.

'You mean nice music might put them to sleep? Good thinking, Milo. I'll do it. I'll do a real slow, sad one. What about "The

Fields of Athenry"'?'

At the first screeching blast of the off-key mouth organ, Eulalia and Mellie stopped eating to stare at Shane. At the next bunch of rum notes he played, their mouths dropped wide open with amazement. When the next notes continued to attack our ears, Mellie and Eulalia had tears streaming down their cheeks.

I'd love to say that they were both entranced by music that they'd never heard before. But my real hope was that Shane's squealing-pig sort of tune would send them running. As if! Those tears were not for the sad tune. The two hags were howling with laughter.

'Hey, cut that out!' I snapped.

'Yes indeed,' said Mister Lewis. 'The poor chap is doing his best.'

It was then I heard another noise. Was

it my imagination or was I hearing faint footsteps coming up the winding stairs?

'Hide behind my chair, boys,' Mister Lewis whispered softly, just before going invisible.

If only we could disappear too! Me and Shane squashed together, listening to the footsteps on the creaky stairs coming closer. We clung to each other when we heard what was left of the door being kicked in.

I don't know what I was expecting, but I was surprised when a small girl stepped into the room. Like some nerdy geek, I shut my eyes tight to block out whatever Eulalia and Mellie might decide to do to her. Call me a coward, but trying to do battle with them to save her was not high in my mind.

'What are you two fools doing in here?' said a cross voice that certainly didn't belong to either of the two hags.

Peering through my fingers, I did a double-take when I saw the women cowering away from the small girl.

'You two clean up this mess, you hear? Oh, and tell me, sisters, where are the horses? I have not seen the beauties on my journey back.'

'We were hungry,' muttered Eulalia.

'Starving,' put in Mellie.

'Did you hear that?' Shane spluttered. 'It was them!'

Before I could stop him, he jumped up and ran like a raging bull towards the two old crones and the little girl, bellowing at the top of his voice, 'Did you two *eat* the horses?'

CHAPTER EIGHTEEN

THE GHOSTLING

Of course I had to chase after him; he's my best mate and you have to look out for your best mate – even when he makes a total ass of himself by barging into a coven of shouting dead women and a thorny little whatever-she-was. Passing me out, with a top-gear waft, came Mister Lewis, waving his gloved hands about and trying to soothe everybody.

'QUIET!' shrieked the small girl. 'What is

happening here? I've been to visit my father's blood kinfolk and I come back to all this.' She waved her arm round the room and glared at Shane, myself and Mister Lewis. 'And who are you?' she snarled, pointing to Mister Lewis.

'Ah,' he answered, raising his hat. 'Lewis, my dear. Dead over a hundred years.'

'And you two,' she pointed at Shane and me. 'When did you die?'

'Die?' exclaimed Shane, grabbing my arm. 'Are we dead, Milo?'

'No, lad,' said Mister Lewis. 'The little lady is just ...'

'Don't "little lady" me!' said the girl, poking Mister Lewis's tummy. 'I am Tara.'

'I beg your pardon, Tara, my dear,' began Mister Lewis.

That earned him another poke in the belly.

'I am not anyone's dear,' she snapped.

I'm a pretty easy-going chap, my mother tells me, like when she wants something done, but I was not going to allow that spitfire ghostling talk like that to my good friend. 'Whoa there, kid,' I said with the lowest growl I could muster. 'Mister Lewis is a gentleman, so you watch your mouth.'

The deadly silence and the shocked, terrified faces made me wish I'd kept my tongue inside my mouth.

The spitfire looked at me and I waited for boxed ears or a well-appointed kick. 'All right,' she said, holding out her hand to a stunned Mister Lewis. 'I am Tara.'

Everyone let out a breath. Then Tara made her sisters pick up the debris of squashed cakes. I could see that Shane wanted to hold on to them, but even he wouldn't dare cross Tara. Just before they left through the broken door, Eulalia turned back and gave us the most evil glare, like a witch chewing a sour lemon.

'Well, that went very well,' said Mister Lewis when we were on our own again, pushing chairs and cardboard against the broken door to keep out the draught.

The candles were sputtering as me and Shane snuggled under a quilt that Mister Lewis had given us. He said he didn't need it because wind went through him anyway. He was just happy to talk to his scared bees, calming them down.

'Mister Lewis is right, Milo. That all went very well,' whispered Shane, tucking his mouth organ under his cushion.

'I hope so,' I muttered as the last of the candles gave up, the cheap torch batteries died and darkness fell. Most of all, I hoped that the women wouldn't come back through the broken door for their revenge. I wished I could be like Shane, who would probably sleep like a baby even if aliens were to sweep down from space and zap him up to an icy cold planet.

CHAPTER NINETEEN

A GARDA VISIT

We got up late in the morning. Mister Lewis offered us some honey, but we declined now that we'd seen up close how the bees make it. Anyway, we had to get to school.

We tip-toed past the ghostly sisters' door, and nobody jumped out at us. They'd probably been out spooking all night.

It felt so good to be out in the morning sun and to breathe in the fresh air that went all the way down to the bottom of our lungs. Even going to school felt good, though we hadn't done our homework, and we were late because there hadn't been anyone to waken us. Across the field we could see that the horses were back on their own territory. Shane wanted to count them to make sure they were all there, but that would have taken ages. When we came towards the school gate, there was a Garda car outside.

'Oh, oh,' muttered Shane. 'Are we in trouble, Milo?'

'I hope my dad isn't there,' I groaned.

Hope wasn't listening to me just then because Dad *was* there, standing beside Mrs Riley, the school principal, interrogating Wedge and Crunch in the empty schoolyard. We nipped over the wall to hide in the bicycle shed.

'We didn't do it,' Wedge was protesting.

'We never went near those horses.'

'Yeah, we were there, but we did nothing,' Crunch protested.

'There were raggy people throwing stones at us from the bushes,' put in Wedge. 'I bet they were the ones who stole our sword. We paid two euro for that, didn't we, Crunch? They'd be the ones you should be looking for. And our pirate flag is missing too.'

'Hold it there, lads! You were seen running from the field,' said Dad.

'That's because we were scared,' Crunch whinged.

'Scared of what?' asked Mrs Riley, her anger making her moustache wobble.

'Of the ghost—' Crunch began, until Wedge nudged him in the ribs.

'A ghost *and* raggy people?' Dad said with a laugh. 'Now I've heard everything. And, by the way, you were also seen fishing from Mister Looney's old boat and now it's missing. Come on, you two. You have a lot of explaining to do.'

'NO! Hang on a sec, Dad!' I shouted, running from the shed.

'Milo?' Dad looked at me. 'What's all this ...?'

'They didn't do it, Dad.'

'And how do you know this, son?'

I knew by Dad's face he was thinking that Wedge and Crunch had some sort of hold over me and Shane. Which I suppose they had, but I couldn't see them taking the flak for something they didn't do.

'Well, they *were* fishing in an old boat in the river,' I said.

'That's right,' added Shane, having got over his amazement of me taking sides with two thugs.

'Then they went home,' I said. 'The boat

was there after they left. Shane and me hung around there for a good while, Dad,' I went on. 'We saw them later going to the cinema.'

'That's the honest truth, Guard,' said Crunch. 'My ma would've clobbered me if I was home late.'

Dad looked at me again. 'Are you sure about this, Milo?'

'It's true, Dad. I'd be the first to tell you if they messed with the horses, and why would they take the boat away from where they fish?'

'Fair enough, son,' said Dad. 'I'll take your word for it.'

'Right, you boys,' sighed Mrs Riley, looking slightly miffed that she wasn't getting rid of Wedge and Crunch after all. 'Back to your classes.'

'What has made you two late for school?' Dad asked as he got into the Garda car.

I struggled to come up with an answer, but it was Dad who provided one. 'I bet it was because Big Ella cooked up a big breakfast for you after your sleepover and you were dawdling along to school.' He laughed as he switched on the ignition.

'Whew, that was close,' I sighed as Dad drove away.

There was a man talking to the class when we went in. He stopped speaking and everyone turned to look at us.

'You're late, you two,' said Miss Lee. 'Sit down and listen to Mister Sullivan. He is the new football coach while Mister Dunne is away.'

I groaned and rested my head on my arms.

'Oh shoot,' Shane whispered to me. 'If I'd known there was to be more bloomin' football, I'd have stayed with the hags in the mill.'

CHAPTER TWENTY

STARS OF THE FUTURE

We didn't see Mister Lewis during the next two days because our class had football training in the yard after school. Shane told Miss Lee that he had 'a wicked bad muscle on his left leg'. And then he sat back and gave me a smarmy grin. Why hadn't I thought of that? He parked himself on the school wall while the rest of us were marched out to the yard for the first bit of training. How he gloated at me as we were made to do all the boring exercises like running up and down like a herd of donkeys and doing those up-and-down squats that make your legs scream. The more pained my face was, the more Shane's belly shook with laughter whenever I glanced his way.

'OK, lads,' said Mister Sullivan finally as he clapped his hands. 'That's good going for your first day. Tomorrow you'll work with footballs. Be sure to bring your soccer gear.'

'Ha!' Shane laughed when we were walking home from school, and my legs were totally screaming with pain. 'Poor Milo. Why didn't you say you had a sore leg – oh no!' He patted my shoulder. 'I'd already picked that one. Tough luck. Never mind,' he went on, 'I'll always be there to cheer you on and buy you a soothing ice-cream on the way home.'

His words went right up my nose and, in spite of my aching muscles, I chased after him. When he turned around to taunt me, he almost ran into Miss Lee coming out of the bookshop.

'Ah, Shane,' she said, holding his shoulder. 'How is that "wicked" leg?'

'Very s-s-sore, Miss,' he stuttered.

'You poor thing,' Miss Lee tut-tutted. 'Which leg is giving you such pain?'

Shane looked down at his legs, trying to figure out the 'sore' one. Even I remembered it was the left, but Shane is the type who says things and then forgets what he said. Just like now.

'This one, Miss,' he said, doing a big limp on his right leg. 'Or maybe it's the other one,' he went on when he saw me shaking my head.

'Ah, so the bad leg is better then,' Miss Lee smiled.

'No, eh, yes,' Shane continued, making a right ass of himself.

'A miracle, Shane.' Miss Lee laughed.

'Yes, Miss,' Shane muttered, still looking at his legs as if he'd never seen them before.

'Well, isn't that wonderful!' Miss Lee continued. 'Now you'll be able to play football with the rest of the class tomorrow.'

CHAPTER TWENTY-ONE

BIG ELLA'S PLAN

A few days later, when we went as usual to Shane's house after school, we were delighted to see Mister Lewis sitting on the sofa with his gloved hands curled around a mug of hot chocolate.

'What's up, Mister Lewis?' asked Shane, straight to the point as usual. 'Your mouth is hanging down. Is it those women, huh? They still bothering you?'

'What women?' asked Big Ella, coming

through from the kitchen with a plate of sandwiches.

Oops! There was a silence.

'Eh,' began Mister Lewis.

'Em,' I muttered.

'A bad lot of crones who are bothering Mister Lewis,' said Shane, even though we weren't supposed to mention Mister Lewis's screechy neighbours.

'Go on,' said Big Ella, setting down the teapot. 'Do tell.'

Well, when Big Ella says 'do something', you do it. So bit by bit we told her about the women who had Mister Lewis in a knot of fear and were probably the raggy people who threw stones at Wedge and Crunch. As we were speaking, Big Ella glanced sympathetically at Mister Lewis as he sank lower and lower in his chair.

'Well, I'm glad I asked,' she said when we

had told her everything, including how the women ate all her snacks and cakes because they hadn't eaten decent food for four hundred years.

'My cakes?' she bellowed. 'The cheek! Tell me what they look like, these mischief-makers?'

'They wear pirate hats,' said Shane.

'Filthy clothes,' I added.

'They look scary,' said Mister Lewis with a shiver.

'Right,' said Big Ella. 'At the weekend we'll go and put those madams in their place.'

'NO, Gran!' Shane spluttered through his biscuit. 'They're horrible. They'll scare you to death and I'll have to live here by myself and become a lonely old geezer like Mister Lewis!'

'You wash your mouth out, boy,' snapped

Big Ella. 'Nobody gets the better of Big Ella. Right?'

'Right,' muttered Shane.

Then Mister Lewis put in his spoke. 'The boy is right, my dear,' he sighed. 'Nobody could tame these women.'

'Excuse me!' said Big Ella, her eyes blazing. '*I'm* a woman and I know how to handle them. Now, you lot, tell me everything.'

And so we did as she asked, right down to the women's filthy clothes and scruffy hair.

Mister Lewis got up from his chair reluctantly. 'I had better go,' he sighed.

'Don't you worry about a thing, my friend,' said Big Ella, brushing down Mister Lewis's dusty coat, which made us all cough. 'Those upstarts will feel the wrath of Big Ella.'

Mister Lewis doffed his hat before wafting off to his miserable home.

'Gran,' said Shane, carefully. 'Are you sure

you can help Mister Lewis ...?'

'Look at me, boy,' she said. 'Have you ever seen me fear anything? Ever?'

'Well, not since the time you freaked out when that spider with hairy legs and shiny eyes—' began Shane.

'Shush, boy,' said Big Ella. 'That's different.'

★

I did everything to stay up late that night so that I wouldn't have nightmares. All that talk of those horrible women and the thoughts of going back to the mill, even with Big Ella, had totally freaked me out. I even asked to wait until Dad came home from night duty, but Mum insisted. 'Now that you're back playing soccer,' she said proudly, 'you'll need all the sleep you can get. You look at all those rich soccer players. They go to bed really early so that they'll be well fit for their matches and make stacks of money.'

'Mum,' I said. 'I'm not a baby. I know what they do and going to bed early is not one of them. I've seen their photos in your magazines.'

She laughed and ruffled my hair, just like she used to do when I was a kid. I wished I was that kid and that there were no spooks of any kind in my life.

'Don't forget to close your window,' she called out. 'I had to open it because I got the smell of socks from the landing.'

That could only mean one thing.

CHAPTER TWENTY-TWO

A SURPRISE VISITOR

'I know you're here,' I whispered.

'Ah, Milo, lad,' said Mister Lewis, stepping out of the wardrobe. 'I just thought I'd, eh, slip over for a chat.'

'They annoyed you again, didn't they?' I said. 'Those women.'

He shrugged his skinny shoulders. 'It's the small one,' he sighed. 'Now that there's no door she keeps coming into my place because she says her sisters are too loud. She looks through my books and talks to my poor, tired bees. And,' he added, 'she constantly asks if there's any chance of getting food like her sisters had been eating. She never shuts up, Milo.'

'Well, let's sleep on it, Mister Lewis,' I yawned, going over to close the window.

'WAAGH!' I yelled, jumping back.

Tara's creepy, beaming face at the window caused me to fall down in shock.

'I followed the old man,' she laughed, climbing into the room. 'What manner of place is this?' she asked, running around like a demented spinning top. She bounced on the bed, waving her tacky pirate hat, then pressed the button on my bedside lamp on and off several times before the bulb blew.

'Hush, girl,' Mister Lewis whispered. 'This is Milo's home.'

'How many families live here?' she asked.

'Just me and my mum and dad,' I hissed. 'Now please get down and be quiet.'

'What is a mum-and-dad?' she asked.

Trying to catch her was like trying to land a slippery eel – not that I've ever tried that, but you know what I mean. In a flash, she was out the door and humming her way down the stairs.

'Stop her, Mister Lewis! FLY!' I hissed, taking the stairs two at a time.

Tara had just reached the half-open door of the lounge and was about to step inside.

'Ah, got you,' sighed Mister Lewis as he grabbed her with his gloved hands and pulled her away from the door. I ran in instead. Mum was sitting on the sofa, looking puzzled. 'Oh, it's you, Milo,' she said. 'I could have sworn I saw a tatty little girl with a hat standing at the door.'

'Maybe you were falling asleep and, eh, got mixed up with telly and reality,' I said.

'Maybe you're right,' she said, still looking puzzled. 'I may even have dozed off. So, what has brought you downstairs?'

This called for quick thinking. 'A hug, Mum. I forgot to give you a goodnight hug.'

CHAPTER TWENTY-THREE

AN UNEXPECTED TRAINING SESSION

'That new soccer coach is dead cool, isn't he, Milo?' Shane asked on our way home from practice a few days later. 'You know,' he went on, 'I think I might get to like soccer.'

'Yeah, it's OK,' I said. 'We're still rubbish, though.'

'No, we're not,' Shane hotly declared. 'We're doing pretty good.'

Well, the biggest surprise came the next day when Mister Sullivan announced that we'd have a trial match to pick a team to play against Saint Mel's in a week's time.

'Great,' said Willie Jones. 'We'll get to go to that posh place where sixth class went. Do we get to stay over too?'

'No,' said Mister Sullivan. 'It's our turn to host a match.'

'Aww,' moaned Willie. 'Count me out.'

'I was going to do that anyway, Willie,' said Mister Sullivan, grinning. 'Running *away* from the ball doesn't score any points for us.'

Well, two days later, Mister Sullivan tried us out on the soccer pitch. I laughed when Shane's name was called out. I didn't laugh when my name was called.

'But I'm useless. Really, I am, Mister Sullivan,' I protested.

'You'll do, Milo,' he grinned. 'Always look at the upside, not the downside.'

Shane said we should practise our moves, so, after school, we fetched his soccer ball, which had hardly ever been used, and headed to the pitch. I just couldn't get over his enthusiasm. Two days ago, he had even bribed me with Big Ella's chocolate biscuits to watch a couple of matches on telly with him.

'Oh no,' he muttered when we came near the pitch. 'This is all we need – not!'

Coming down the road towards us were Wedge and Crunch.

'Hide the ball, Milo,' said Shane, shoving it into my hands.

'Hide it where, Shane?'

'Up your jumper. Quick!'

Did he really think they wouldn't notice skinny me with a sudden big belly like his?

'Oh darn it,' he muttered, 'they've seen us. Brace yourself, Milo.'

That was easy for him to say now that I was the one holding the ball. Running away wasn't an option.

'Perhaps if we avoid eye contact, they'll just pass by,' Shane whispered.

'Hey,' the two bullies said together.

'Hey,' we said back.

'Nice ball,' said Crunch.

'Are you guys on the junior soccer team?' asked Wedge.

'Yes, we are,' Shane answered defensively, waiting for the jeers and insults.

'You must be good so,' went on Wedge.

'No, we're not.' I felt I had to say it before they would. 'We're rubbish.' There, I thought, those two would have no stinging words to throw at us now because we did it ourselves.

'Speak for yourself,' Shane hissed in my ear until he realised what I was trying to do.

'Yeah?' asked Crunch.

'Yeah,' I replied. 'Total rubbish.' Now maybe they'd leave us alone and go away.

'We could give you a few tips,' said Wedge. 'Come on and we'll have a few kicks around.'

Oh shoot! My great plan flopped like a pigeon's poo.

'Nice one, Milo,' Shane hissed in my ear as we followed them. 'We're dead.'

I knew that, but there was no turning back now. I shut my eyes for three seconds and wished for a load of guys to surge in for a game – then we'd have to leave. Needless to say, my message didn't get to whoever looks after wusses like me and Shane up in the clouds. We kicked the ball around for a couple of minutes. Then Wedge came over to me. I braced myself for whatever was going to happen.

'Where will you be playing?' he asked.

'Here in the field,' I began. What was I saying? I was really asking for it.

'I mean what position?'

'Oh, centre field where Mister Sullivan says I can't do much wrong.'

'Good,' Wedge nodded. 'And what would you do if you saw a guy charging at you with the ball at his feet?'

'I'd get it off him,' I said.

'No, you wouldn't,' snorted Shane.

'Yes, he would,' put in Wedge. 'Listen, kid,' he said, pulling me towards him. 'Almost all blokes can only kick with their right foot, OK?'

I nodded my head.

'So, you stay on the right side. The guy

with the ball will pretend to go left, but you stay on the right.'

'And what position are you, big guy?' asked Crunch.

Shane ignored the half-insult. 'I'm the goalie. So far my average is six goals a game,' he muttered.

'So what will you do when a forward comes towards you with the ball at his feet?' Crunch asked.

'I usually jump up and down to put him off. It has never worked,' answered Shane.

'Next time,' said Crunch, 'step out a few feet from the goal-line to narrow the angle and be ready to dive at his feet.'

'Yeah?'

'Yeah, dive at his feet. Wait until he is just going to shoot. No problem. Right?'

'Huh, no problem at all then,' Shane chuckled.

'So,' said Wedge. 'We're quits now. Best of luck, GIRLS!'

'Yeah, right!' laughed Crunch as they sprinted away.

CHAPTER TWENTY-FOUR

BIG ELLA INTO ACTION

Mum and Dad were going to the cinema that night, and Big Ella insisted that I stay at her place.

'The boys can help me with a few chores,' she told Mum.

That didn't sound great, but at least there'd be the reward of a bun or two.

She was packing big boxes into the boot

of her car when Shane and I got there after the football practice. 'Ah,' she said. 'You're just in time, boys, to carry the rest of the stuff.'

'What's all this stuff for, Gran?' Shane asked.

'We're going to the mill,' she replied.

Shane and I groaned.

'Can't Mister Lewis come to our house like he always does?' asked Shane.

Big Ella just smiled. Shane and me knew that once she decides on something there's no stopping her.

We did as she asked and packed boxes into the boot, and what didn't fit there we squashed into the back seat with us.

'What's with all the boxes? Are we going to stay in the mill, Gran?' Shane asked nervously.

'Don't be daft, child.' She laughed. 'I just have a few things to put right.'

When Big Ella parked the car at the bridge, we hauled all those boxes through the field to the mill and wished we had the trolley that Mister Lewis had nicked.

Then we struggled upstairs and through the makeshift door.

'It's alright, Mister Lewis,' I said when I saw dust rising. 'It's just us and Big Ella.'

'Ah,' he said, as he came together. 'I'm afraid you've come at a bad time, Big Ella. I was just about to clean up another mess.'

'No worries, Mister Lewis,' she replied. 'It's not you I have come to see. Now, tell me, where are these ladies who cause you so much trouble?'

CHAPTER TWENTY-FIVE

CRISIS MEETING

When Mister Lewis told Big Ella more stories about the carry-on of his shrieking neighbours, she tut-tutted and shook her head. Once, she even sighed sadly and said, 'The poor dears.'

'Poor dears, my eye,' said Mister Lewis indignantly. 'They come in here and trash the place, looking for my food. Nightmares, that's what they are.'

'I knew there was something up at the

mill,' Big Ella said as she patted Mister Lewis's gloved hand. 'Every time you've come to my house recently, you've seemed to shrink a bit more. We'll sort all this out, trust me. There have been incidents of the walking dead in Africa. I've brought several things that might help. So, boys,' she said, getting up from her chair, 'let's have a cup of tea while we wait to meet these three and put them right.'

But Mister Lewis was shaking his head.

'It won't work, Big Ella,' he sighed. 'They will just come back and trash it all again.'

Big Ella put her pudgy hands on her big hips. 'They'll be dealing with *me*,' she said in a tone of voice that would cut through a fridge. 'Let's set the table for tea.'

She opened the boxes and put out plates of buns, chocolate biscuits and two different kinds of cakes.

'Wow!' said Shane, reaching out towards the buns.

'Not yet, Shane,' said Big Ella.

'Why, Gran?

'Trust me, lad,' she smiled. 'We must wait for our guests.'

'What guests?' asked Shane. 'You don't mean ...?' he spluttered.

'You wouldn't!' said Mister Lewis, his face like putty again.

I said nothing because my teeth were locked with fear.

It wasn't long before we heard the screeching sisters, back from their mischief.

The shrill shouting stopped when they came into our room.

'What is happening here, old man?' Eulalia snarled. 'And who is this big dark-faced woman ...?'

Mellie was shaking her head, and tiny

Tara was eying me and Shane with an impish grin. Then they saw the food and the three of them made a dash towards the table, Eulalia waving a gaudy silver sword at Big Ella. Big Ella folded her huge arms and stood before them.

'Not so much as a morsel will you have until you learn manners,' she said. Eulalia and Mellie laughed and took another step forward, pulling Tara along. Big Ella barred them, her big body wider than the three sisters together. She snatched the sword from Eulalia and snapped it in two. Then she grabbed Eulalia and pushed her face right up to hers.

'Not one more step, my dear,' she said in a low, menacing voice as she put her hand in her pocket and produced a small, hideous African head. 'This,' she said slowly, 'is the shrunken head of my dead ancestor, whose magic powers have come to me. My anger towards you is mighty! You are not good people.'

Well, that certainly stopped the sisters — as well as scaring the wits out of me and Shane. Eulalia and Mellie backed away. Tara stood her ground, her eyes focused on the head. 'Will you really set that spirit upon us?' she whispered.

'Indeed I shall, and much worse,' replied Big Ella, 'if you three refuse to repair all the damage you have done to Mister Lewis. And another thing,' she roared on. 'Was it you lot who frightened the poor horses away?

'Yes, it was them,' said Tara. 'I told them not to.'

'What *are* you two? Are you some sort of female rustlers?'

'We are river pirates,' said Eulalia proudly, touching her battered pirate hat.

'River pirates? Pah!' laughed Tara. 'You two are river cowards who hide in the bushes and throw stones at people who are fishing or just out walking.'

'Then they must be the ones who stole the little boat. Wedge and Crunch were blamed for that,' I said.

'No, that was me,' said Tara. 'I hid it so that they couldn't sink it. So,' she said to her sisters as she stood beside Big Ella, 'some river pirates you two have turned out to be. River scarecrows, more like.'

'Enough of this!' yelled Big Ella. 'We're all going to clean up Mister Lewis's home and make it comfortable.'

'Oh dear,' said Mister Lewis. 'I can look after all that ...'

'No, dear,' said Big Ella. 'You're very stressed, so the ones who caused that must be the ones to help us fix it.'

'That's fair,' Tara agreed. 'Come here, sisters,' she hollered.

'Only if that big lady puts away the shrunken head,' cried Eulalia.

'Done,' said Big Ella. 'He will be in my pocket all the time – unless there's trouble, of course. Come and help.'

'What about those cakes, Gran?' asked Shane.

'We shall all eat them together nicely when the work is done,' Big Ella replied.

'We have to wait that long?' protested Mellie.

'After we've all washed,' said Big Ella.

Well, that sent Shane and me into the battle. Everyone was shouting at the same time.

'QUIET! Will you all be quiet, PLEASE!'

'Ah, Mister Lewis,' smiled Big Ella. 'At last you have found your *real* voice again. Do hold on to it. Now, to work everyone.'

'Gran,' Shane whispered nervously as Big Ella handed paintbrushes to us, 'that shrunken head thing, is it real?'

'Of course not, luv,' she chuckled. 'I picked it up in the charity shop.'

CHAPTER TWENTY-SIX

UP FOR THE MATCH

Shane kept telling me that I was a wuss on the day of our match. I'd already puked twice, once on Mum's new rug in the hall and later in the kitchen when I got the whiff of Dad's sausages frying in the pan. Mum had washed my soccer gear and she even ironed it. 'I went to a lot of trouble,' she said. 'So no more vomiting please.'

'I know, Mum,' I sighed.

'Oh, I'm joking, Milo,' she laughed, giving me a hug that almost did stir up more puke. 'I'm so proud of you. Dad and I will be there to cheer for you. I'll be waving my red scarf.'

'Great, Mum. Just don't scream my name, OK?'

I called in for Shane, who wasn't even remotely nervous. I've always wished I was as cool as him. He said that in Africa no one gets their knickers in a knot over games because they're used to worse things like vicious crocodiles, fanged snakes and plants that eat people. I don't know where he got that information because he was only a baby when he and his granny came to Ireland.

'Cakes are for later, fellas,' Big Ella said when Shane reached out, as he was leaving, for a scone with raspberry jam.

'Good luck, boys,' said Mister Lewis, all chirpy and back to his old self. 'I'll be there.'

We walked to the soccer pitch because Shane said it was another way to get noticed. He reckoned that there might be soccer guys hanging around scouting for kids like us that they'd take back to England for top-notch training. And we'd be put up in hotels so posh that we could just snap our fingers for anything we want.

'Shane,' I laughed. 'This is our first ever match. Except for the tips we got from Wedge and Crunch, we barely know what to do.'

'You kick the ball,' said Shane, 'and I'll stop it.'

'But I'll be kicking to *the other* goal,' I said.

'Oh yeah, you're right,' grinned Shane.

'Huh, where did those two come from?' he added when he saw Wedge and Crunch waiting at the sideline.

'Hey, Shane,' grinned Wedge. 'Haven't you forgotten something?'

'What?' asked Shane.

'Your SKIRT!' chortled Crunch.

They both shut up when they saw Dad coming towards us to wish us luck.

'Give 'em stick, guys,' he called out to Shane and me. 'Bend it like … like, eh … Pelé.'

I cringed when Wedge and Crunch and even Shane sniggered. Dad is big on rugby but knows nothing about soccer. Shane would hoot about this for days.

Dad turned to Wedge and Crunch. 'It looks like you two are in the clear,' he said. 'The missing boat was found farther down the river. Probably broke its moorings.'

But Crunch was looking over Dad's shoulder, his grin disappearing as the three pirate sisters came over the hill.

'Hey, Mister ... I mean, Guard!' he shouted after Dad. 'There's the raggedy women who were throwing stones at us. Go on, arrest them.'

But Dad was already out of earshot.

Like a mini whirlwind, Tara came screaming towards Wedge and Crunch, waving her broken sword that was held together with one of Big Ella's stockings. 'Who are you calling raggedy?' she shrilled. 'Look at me. I'm lovely!'

I'm not much interested in whatever girls wear, you understand, though I had to admit she did look different.

However, the shouts from Wedge cut through any silly thoughts about girls with hair and frocks. He pointed at the sword. 'That's ours,' he snarled so fiercely that little spits flew from his lips. 'You stole our sword, thief!'

Tara made a run at Wedge. 'I am NOT a thief,' she yelled. 'I'm the PIRATE COUSIN of GRANUAILE,' she added dramatically.

'Ha!' put in Crunch. 'That Graniathingy one is dead for years.'

'And so are me and my sisters,' retorted Tara, pointing to Eulalia and Mellie.

Wedge and Crunch took to their panicky heels, followed by Tara, waving the plastic sword and being cheered on by her sisters.

'Wow!' I said to Shane. 'Have you ever heard anyone as loud as those women?'

'Ha, Milo,' laughed Shane. 'When Big Ella was shampooing their hair, they screamed like banshees.'

★

When we were all sent out onto the pitch, after a talk from Mister Sullivan, I was glad I'd had no breakfast to throw up. The whistle blew and we were off.

I hardly got to kick the ball during the match, but I did what Wedge and Crunch had said. Every time I went to an opposition's right side, they kicked the ball against my legs and it mostly rebounded to one of our own players. We even scored a goal after one of my 'passes'. My legs were black and blue, but I was so proud it didn't matter.

'Shane, my man,' I said gallantly after the final whistle blew, 'you were the star of the show. And when you dived in front of their big forward, that was totally cool.'

Shane rubbed his bruised forehead. 'That was no dive, Milo. Mister Lewis was right behind me, yabbering in my ear. I tried to get out of the way of the forward, but Mister Lewis pushed me at the last second and the ball just hit my head.'

'You mean it was your big head that won

the cup for us?' I laughed. 'Cool, Shane.'

When our team went up to get the cup, I saw Mum waving her red scarf like mad and Dad blowing a horn, and Miss Lee was waving a flag too. Beyond them, I saw three figures also waving, and, instead of screeching, they were laughing. Yes, they were Tara, Mellie and Eulalia, dressed in the vintage clothes that Big Ella had given them – after she'd made them scrub themselves and shampoo their hair. They looked well posh jumping up and down with excitement and chatting to Big Ella.

I was sort of sorry when the sisters told us they were going back through time to their kinfolk in Galway, leaving Mister Lewis in charge of the mill.

'Back to our own time,' said Mellie.

'We've noticed that our snooty upstart

cousin Granuaile gets all the fame,' said Eulalia. 'We intend to change all that.'

'Yes indeed,' added Mellie. 'Watch out for *our* names and faces on books.'

'I just want a nice, quiet life,' sighed Tara. 'No more trying to tame my big sisters.'

When we went back to the dressing room, I turned to Shane. 'Didn't Big Ella say me and Mum and Dad are having tea in your place?'

'Yes, Milo. So hurry up,' he said. 'I'm starving. I'm so hungry I could eat a horse.'

READ MORE MILO ADVENTURES

When Shane's gran digs up a weird
ancient stone, best buddies Milo and
Shane find themselves face to face with
its owner — one dead angry druid.
Willie Jones's lizard goes mental and
Shane disappears. Milo is in deep, deep
trouble, and he needs a rescue plan before
midnight strikes.

MILO AND THE RAGING CHIEFTAINS

Milo's ghostly buddy, Mister Lewis, appears
in the town's ancient castle, but he's not
alone. He's in trouble and needs Milo's help.
Things get very complicated when Milo's
teacher, Miss Lee, accidentally wakes some
raging chieftains from long ago. And then
she disappears.